Stories of the Heart

A Christmas Short Story Collection

J. Adams

ISBN-13: 978-0615545349
ISBN-10: 0615545343

Cover art By Michelle Cruz

To my family

A Season of Miracles

On Christmas Eve morning, Elijah awakened and looked around the large room at all the still-sleeping boys. At ten years old, he was the youngest boy residing at Lexton Orphanage for Boys. Having been abandoned on the front steps of the establishment when he was just a baby, it was the only home he had ever known. Every day Elijah dreamed of finally being adopted, and every night he fell asleep with that same chanted prayer on his lips. He wanted real parents–people who would love him unconditionally and who would look over his imperfect body.

As the six o'clock alarm sounded through the speaker on the wall, Elijah pulled his twisted body out of bed and limped toward the bathroom, but as usual, he was too slow and the stalls were already filled. Elijah had been hit by a car over four years ago when they were taken on an outing in the country to study birds. He loved birds, any and all kinds of birds. But his favorite bird was the white dove. There was just something special about them. It was a white dove he was intently studying and had walked across the road to get a closer look at when he was struck by a speeding car. He had been immediately rushed to the hospital, and after emergency surgery and months of therapy, he was left slightly bent with a prominent limp that he would always have.

After finally finding a spot in the long row of sinks to wash his face, brush his teeth, and comb his hair, he made his way back to his bed and got dressed, being the last to reach the cafeteria. He quickly ate his food and put his try away, then headed to the assembly hall, snagging a second row seat for a change. The administrator had announced that there would be an important presentation following breakfast.

Once all the boys were present in the hall, Mr. Pram, the administrator, stood on the raised platform.

"Today, a large group of married couples will be coming to the orphanage. Each couple will be choosing one of you to adopt and make you a part of their family."

Suddenly the hall was filled with the sound of the boys' excited voices as they talked excitedly amongst themselves. Elijah's voice was not heard among the others, for though his mind and heart were filled with the desperate hope that he would be one of the boys chosen, deep down he worried that no one would want him because of his imperfect body. Still, he would keep the prayer in his heart that he would be blessed with parents that day.

❊ ❊ ❊

That afternoon, the boys were brought into the large gathering hall on the upper floor of the orphanage where the couples were waiting. Elijah scanned the various faces. Some couples were young, some were older, and some were in between. All of them looked nice and Elijah suddenly found himself imagining which couple he would go home with. Despite his doubts, he'd still packed his bag along with the other boys in anticipation of leaving with his new family.

Elijah watched throughout the day as boy after boy left with new parents, his heart falling with each couple that passed him by. By the end of the day he was completely broken. He was the only boy left at the orphanage.

As he lay in bed that night in the large room he now occupied alone, he sobbed into his pillow. It hadn't happened. He hadn't been chosen. He was going to be spending another Christmas there–completely alone.

"Why, God?" he whispered against the damp pillow. "Why did none of them want me? Why does nobody want me?"

"Someone does want you," he heard a voice whisper softly. He opened his eyes and slowly sat up. His eyes widened as they fell on the beautiful woman standing by his bed. She had long blond hair, brilliant green eyes, was completely dressed in white. Her smile was soft and her eyes were kind. She looked like an angel.

"Are you?" Elijah asked the vision in awe. "Are you an angel?"

No," she answered softly. "I am just someone who loves you very much." She moved closer and sat on the bed next to him, and he felt her warmth radiating around him. She smelled like flowers and sunlight. "I know you are lonely and sad and you feel that God is not listening, but He is. This is a season of miracles, Elijah. After all, the birth of God's son was a miracle, and so was His life." She paused. "Do you know the Savior, Elijah?"

Elijah smiled. "I don't know Him, but I know *of* Him."

The woman smiled back. "He knows, you, Elijah. He knows what you are going through and He feels your pain. All the times when you've felt alone, you really haven't been because He has been here with you. She pointed to his chest. "And he has been there in your heart, and He will always be. Don't ever forget that, Elijah. Don't ever doubt it. Promise me."

"I won't," Elijah promised. He felt so much love for the woman in the brief time she had been there, he would promise her anything.

"Now," she said, moving to her knees by his bed, her voice growing even softer, "Lay your head and close your eyes, dear one, for you are special in God's eyes and loved beyond measure. He has ever been mindful of you, just as He is with all of His children, and He has a special Christmas planned for you. I promise. Now sleep."

Smiling with peace radiating in his heart, Elijah lay down and a wave of drowsiness came over him as soon as his head hit the pillow. Before falling asleep, he was almost sure he felt a warm kiss pressed against his cheek and the name David whispered in his ear.

❉ ❉ ❉

On Christmas morning Elijah wore his best shirt as he ate breakfast alone in the large cafeteria. He received a present from the kitchen and cleaning staff, as well as one from Mr. Pram and his secretary. They gave him a new book, a pen and journal, and a small box of fruit, nuts and candy. He knew they all felt bad that he hadn't been adopted along with the rest of the boys, but he wouldn't let them see him down. He smiled cheerfully and thanked them for the gifts, holding onto the wonderful vision he'd been given the night before and the new-found knowledge that he would never be alone.

Later that morning as Elijah sat on his bed reading one of the many classic tales in the thick book he'd received, Mr. Pram came and informed him that someone was there to see him. His heart pounding, he closed the book and followed the administrator down to the parlor that was reserved for important guests. As Elijah entered the room, a man stood. He was tall and wore a neatly pressed suit. There were small streaks of gray in his dark hair, and even with the subtle lines around his eyes, his face looked young. The man nervously held his hat in his hands as he approached Elijah.

"Hello. My name is David Christian." He held out his hand.

The man's voice was deep and kind, even loving, and Elijah immediately felt a sense of comfort just being near him. He timidly shook Mr. Christian's hand.

"I'm sorry about yesterday," the man said. "I meant to be here, but . . . well . . . I didn't know if you would want . . . I was afraid."

Elijah was puzzled. "Afraid of what, sir?"

The man ran a nervous hand through his hair. "I was afraid you wouldn't want to be my son."

Feeling a thrill of excitement at the thought of this kind man being his new father, Elijah asked, "Why did you think that?"

The man knelt down and bowed his head. "Well, you see . . . it was me. I was the person who hit you over four years ago." Tears filled the man's voice and streaked down his face. "You see, I lost my wife that morning. She died giving birth to our son, and he died a few hours later. I was coming from the hospital. I was crying and rubbing a hand over my eyes when you came across the road. I didn't see you, and when I realized that I had hit you, I became hysterical." He paused, wiping his eyes. "For a long time after that, I couldn't cope. I couldn't sleep, I couldn't eat, so I began to drink. Last year I finally became sober. I asked God what I could do to make amends and it came to me that you might still need a parent. So I worked on making myself worthy enough to be a father to you. I was all set to come to talk to you, but at the last minute I got scared." The man finally looked up at Elijah. "Do you think you could find it in your heart to forgive me, maybe even let me be your father?"

Elijah hadn't said a single word during the man's confession. As he listened, all he could think about was the vision of the angelic woman and the promise she made him that this Christmas would be special. And she had been right. He had been given a father. His prayers had been answered. Nothing else mattered.

It felt completely natural for Elijah to lean forward and wrap his arms around the man's neck. "I forgive you, Dad," he said simply. "I forgive you and I'm ready to go home now." He felt and heard the sob that tore from the man's throat as he tightly returned his embrace.

"I didn't think you would be able to forgive me," Mr. Christian said, drawing back and wiping his eyes.

Elijah smiled. "After what the beautiful lady told me last night, I figured you had to be a good man for God to send you to me."

"What lady?" he asked.

"The lady in my vision. She said that God loved me and He had a special Christmas planned for me. She promised. She even said your name. David."

The man's eyes again filled with tears. He pressed a shaky warm hand to Elijah's cheek. "Elijah, what did the lady look like?"

"She had long blond hair, green eyes, and a kind smile. She smelled like flowers." When the man began to cry again, Elijah reached out and touched his face. "What is it, Dad?"

David Christian looked into his his eyes and smiled. "That was my wife, Anne." He wiped his face, then reached up and took Elijah's face in his hands and pressed a kiss to his forehead. "Before Anne died, she said she would watch over our son until we had both healed and it was time for me to receive him. I thought she meant our baby boy, that he would be with her in heaven and she would take care of him until we were together again. Little did I know she was talking about you. She had known–somehow she had known we would need each other."

"Well," Elijah said, smiling widely, "we *do* need each other, and this *is* the season of miracles."

"It is indeed, son. It is indeed."

❄ ❄ ❄

An hour later, Elijah walked out the orphanage doors with his father, shedding his previous life as a cast off, and embracing his new life as a beloved son–a son with both a Heavenly and an earthly father.

It was truly a most excellent Christmas. It was the best, and one he would treasure for the rest of his life.

Simeon's Hands

Once upon a time there was a young woodcarver named Simeon. He lived alone in a small stone cottage on the edge of town that had a little workshop attached. Simeon was gifted and could create anything from wood, and his work was known far and wide. He had no family and not many close friends, but he was happy and he never complained. Business was good and he had everything he needed.

Christmas was soon approaching and it was announced throughout the land that the king would be hosting a grand party on Christmas Eve. It was required that each guest bring a gift to present to the king.

Simeon loved the king and wanted to create a special present for him, something unlike anything he'd ever done before, something that would show his love for the king. He thought and pondered for a while and an idea formed in his head. The design was so clear, he immediately wanted to get started.

He walked through the woods behind his cottage and searched for the perfect piece of wood. Finding a fallen maple tree, he chopped off a thick log, placed it on his shoulder, and walked back to his shop.

That afternoon, a rich merchant entered the shop and commissioned a grand piece to be made for him to give to the king.

"I want it to be something that has never been done before," said the man. "It should be a gift fit for a king."

Simeon immediately thought about the gift he was creating to give to the king himself. If he gave it to the man, he would not have a gift for the king himself and he knew he wouldn't be able to come up with another carving as grand as the one he was working on.

Since Christmas was about sharing and putting others before oneself, Simeon decided to finish the carving and give it to the merchant. It would be a sacrifice, but he would do it. He had been given a gift of creating beauty with his hands and he would not be selfish. He would just have to create another gift to give to the king.

❄ ❄ ❄

Simeon spent the rest of the day cutting the wood down and shaping it, preparing it for carving. He took his time, feeding his love and care into the wood, hoping the king would feel it as well when he looked at the finished piece. He worked through the night, smiling as applied the first carvings. Just before dawn, he entered the cottage, lay on his bed, closed his eyes, and slept a few hours until it was time to open the shop.

Exiting his home to go into the wood shop, Simeon smelled smoke. He looked down the road and saw people pointing to a barn that had caught fire. Simeon ran down the road and saw the elderly owner trying to get his animals out. He immediately ran in and found a lamb trapped in a corner of the barn. Fire surrounded the small animal.

Simeon ran through the fire and swatted at the flame that caught the leg of his pants. He took off his thick wool shirt and wrapped it around the lamb, then ran back through the flame, gasping in pain as the flames lapped against the backs of his hands.

The man cried as Simeon exited the barn and placed the lamb in his arms. He thanked the young woodcarver for saving the animal, then a neighbor immediately tended to his burned hands. Simeon shed tears as he looked at his hands. He knew they would never be the same.

For two weeks Simeon gritted his teeth through the pain of his burned hands and worked on carving the piece, but he could not get his hands to work the way he needed them to. He finally placed the tools on the table in defeat and sat on the stool as tears of frustration streamed down his cheeks. How could he possibly finish the gift when it was hard for him to even do the most basic things anymore?

Yet something inside him just would not give up.

❉ ❉ ❉

The day before the royal party, the merchant who had commissioned the gift for the king came back to the shop to pick it up. When Simeon presented him with the carving the man became angry.

"What is the meaning of this?" he yelled. "Where is the grand piece you promised me?"

"But sir," Simeon said, "I have tried, but my hands no longer work the same. I am sorry." The man turned up his nose.

"Yes, well your apology is too little too late. Now what am I supposed to give the king?" When the woodcarver lowered his head in shame, the man shook his head and said, "I will never be back to your shop." He promptly turned and left.

Simeon went back over to the carving and picked it up, holding it close to his heart as his tears trailed down his face and dropped upon the wood. There was no other choice. He would have to give it to the king anyway and hope his majesty would not throw him out for bringing an unfinished, deformed gift.

❋ ❋ ❋

By the time Simeon arrived the next evening, the ballroom of the palace was completely full. The king sat upon his throne in all his magnificent splendor and Simeon felt awed to be in his presence. The guests began presenting their gifts to the king. One by one they approached and each gift opened was more beautiful than the next. The eyes of each guest were filled with pride at the king's reaction to their gift.

Finally it was Simeon's turn to approach the king with his covered gift, but he found that his feet would not move. He was afraid and filled with shame for bringing something so unworthy of the king. He was about to turn and leave when he heard the king say, "Come, Simeon."

Surprised and awed that the king knew his name, he slowly approached the throne. When he reached the throne, the king stood. Simeon's scarred hands shook as the king uncovered the gift.

The room became silent.

After another moment, the guest began to murmur. "How could he be so impertinent as to bring his majesty something so unworthy? How could he even show his face with such a hideous gift? What insolence!" The murmurs were numerous.

Then the guests observed the king and the murmuring ceased.

The king lovingly caressed the figurine as tears fell down his face onto the wood. He looked into Simeon's eyes. "This is the most beautiful gift I have ever received. No one in the kingdom has ever given so much of himself."

When Simeon stared at the king in disbelief, the king said, "Shall I tell you what I see when I look at your gift?" Not waiting for an answer he continued. "I see my image, dressed in luxurious splendor. I see each and every fold of the flowing robe. I see the shimmer of my graying, shoulder-length hair, the strength of my shoulders, and the clarity of my eyes. I see each point of the golden crown upon my head."

He reached out and pressed a gentle hand to Simeon's face. "But most of all, I see the devotion in the eyes of the boy kneeling by my side as he looks up at me. I see the radiance of his smile. I see the valiance of his soul. And as I take in the blood stains here and there on the wood, I see the love and sacrifice that went into this creation. So truly, my son, this is the greatest gift I have ever received."

Simeon smiled, joy radiating from his soul, for everything the king saw was exactly what he pictured when he began the figurine. How could the king have seen it? How could he see the intended beauty in the disfigured piece of wood?

Reading Simeon's mind, the king said, "I simply see the beauty that radiates from you." The king immediately ordered that the guests be sent away. When the room was cleared, he placed the figurine on the floor and took Simeon's scarred hand in his.

"Of all the gifts I've received tonight from my guests, you were the only one who truly knew me. You did not give me a gift to impress me. Your gift was one of love and it came from your heart. And because of your loving sacrifice, I invite you to live here with me as my son. Everything I have is yours, including all my power." The king released his hands.

Feeling a tingling sensation, Simeon looked at his hands and gasped. They were healed! The scars were gone and his hands were whole again. He looked at the king, the love in his heart completely filling him. "How can I ever repay you for giving so much to someone as unworthy as myself?"

The king smiled. "You are worth more than all the treasures of the earth, my son. And now, not only will the world know it, but you will as well."

So from that day forward, the young woodcarver dwelt with the king and learned a valuable lesson. He learned that gifts given to impress and gain favor were of no importance, for they were as deceiving as the pride of the giver.

The gifts that were important were ones given in sacrifice, and given from the heart.

A Winter Miracle

Andrew and his family sat with his parents in the family room and gazed at the beautifully decorated Christmas tree, preparing for "Christmas Story Time." Every year they would all come together, each of them prepared to tell a story they made up to share with everyone.

"Who wants to go first?" Grandma asked, excited to hear what her grand kids came up with this year.

"I will!" Sheila, the ten year old said. Then she began her fascinating Christmas tale for this year.

"Wonderful!" Grandma cried and everyone clapped.

Twelve year old Steven was next, followed by Cara and Andrew. Applause was given after each one.

"Okay, Mom, your turn," Andrew said as he turned up his glass of eggnog, emptying it in three swallows. He set the glass down and rubbed his hand together, a look of anticipation in his eyes. He knew it was going to be a good one.

Mom smiled.

"Okay, here we go. Once upon a time, there was a young woman named Kenna . . ."

It was Christmas Eve. Kenna Summer blew into her hands, trying to warm them and let her eyes scan her surroundings. It was below freezing and dark, and she was stranded in the middle of nowhere. She had considered the people she partied with on a regular basis her friends, but they really hadn't been. They had all been drinking, and for a change, Kenna was the sober one. As a joke, on their way back to Grand Junction, the unruly group threw her out of the car and left her there to find her way to the next town–almost forty miles away. She had no coat, and the thick sweater she wore did nothing to warm her against the frigid weather. It had begun to snow and the ground was becoming icy.

Kenna began to cry, her tears freezing against her cheeks as she thought about all the mistakes she'd made that brought her to this point in her life. When both her parents died in a car accident, Kenna's emotions ran wild. She dropped out of her junior year of college and found a new circle of friends. For two years she went from place to place, living a lifestyle that was destructive, both emotionally and spiritually.

Now here she was, twenty-two years old with no job, no home, and at the moment, stranded on a lone road, unable to see anything but the shadows of trees in the thick forest on either side of her.

Feeling completely unworthy and wondering if she would even be answered, she called on God to help her.

"If you're up there," she said, looking up to the heavens, "please help me. I don't know where I am, I'm cold, and I'm afraid. Please help me find my way to someplace safe."

No sooner had Kenna finished her prayer, a dim light appeared deep in the woods. She looked down at her canvas tennis shoes and knew they would be soaked within minutes from the snow, but she also knew she had no choice but to find that light. After all, she *had* prayed for help. She turned and trudged slowly through the woods, feeling the urge to stop because of fatigue, but knowing if she did, she would freeze to death.

After about fifteen minutes, Kenna came to a clearing where a log cabin sat atop a hill with a gravel driveway that stretched out in the opposite direction. The light from the windows radiated a sudden warmth to her bones, making her quicken her pace. She was so exhausted, she fell a couple of times. By he time she made it to the steps of the front porch, her legs couldn't carry her another step and she fell, barely holding onto consciousness.

The front door opened and a man exited. He knelt down, scooped Kenna up in his arms and took her inside. He placed her on the sofa before the fireplace. Kenna opened her eyes at the sound of his deep voice.

"We need to get you warm."

Kenna looked at him. She could tell he was young, maybe twenty-five or thirty at the most. She took in his kind, bearded face, clear blue eyes, and long blond ponytail and asked in a hoarse voice, "Are you an angel?"

The man smiled. "I have been called many things, but angel is not one of them."

"But . . . you must be," Kenna said. Her shivering increased.

The man went and got a couple of thick blankets and covered her with them, then took off her wet shoes and socks. He made a mug of hot chocolate and helped her drink some.

"How did you come to be out here with no coat or boots?" he asked.

Kenna didn't want to answer him, but knew she had no choice. She could never lie to him after he'd shown her so much kindness.

"My friends . . . or my supposed friends, put me out on the side of the road and left." A tear rolled down her cheek. "But I suppose it is no more than I deserve."

"Nobody deserves to be treated so cruelly," he said, wiping the tear with his finger. He encouraged her to take another drink of the chocolate.

Kenna ran a hand back through her tangled, matted hair. She knew what she must look like. Her gaunt cheeks, dirty clothes, and unkempt hair made her look like a starved vagabond. She looked into his kind eyes. "I'm not a good person. I've done things and . . . I . . . I'm . . . I'm not a good person."

The man smiled. "You are better than you think you are. You've been living the harsh parts of life so long that you have just forgotten."

Kenna stifled a sob. "I want to remember . . . I want to be who I was before . . . but I think it is too late for me now."

The man continued to smile, and the warmth of it surrounded Kenna.

"It is never too late."

"Can I ask your name?" Kenna finally said.

He took her now empty cup. "Matthew," he answered.

"I am happy to meet you, Matthew. And I am grateful for your help. Thank you." She looked toward the corner at the small Christmas tree that sat atop a wooden table and guilt instantly rose in her.

"I'm so sorry for ruining your Christmas."

"Hey," Matthew said, taking her small hand between his large, warm ones. "You have only made it better. I think God sent you here to give me someone to spend this holidays with. My nearest neighbor is twenty-five miles away." He smiled. "I was supposed to be here to help you."

Kenna's doubtful eyes filled with tears. "Yeah, and as usual, I have nothing to give back. I never do."

"But you do," Matthew said, touching her face. "This is the season for miracles, so let Christ perform one for you. Give Him your broken heart. Invite Him into your life, give your sorrows to Him and he will send you comfort. It is never too late."

Kenna nodded, then covered her face with her hands and cried more than she had since her parents died. She cried for their loss, and for every poor choice she had ever made.

After a moment, Kenna found herself cradled in the warmth of Matthew's embrace. He was a stranger and yet . . . he didn't seem like a stranger to her. Everything about him seemed familiar. He flannel shirt smelled of cinnamon, vanilla and pine. The scent gave her a feeling of safety.

After a while, Matthew drew back and smiled. "I have a few things my sister left here last year–sweaters, jeans, socks, and a few toiletries. You are thinner that she is, but they just might fit." He stood. "Why don't you go on down the hall to the room on the left and change out of those wet clothes while I bring in some ham from the smokehouse and fix you something to eat."

She looked up at him as tears again filled her eyes. She couldn't seem to stop crying. "You've been so nice to me. I don't deserve it."

Matthew knelt down, again taking her hands in his. "You deserve this and more, much more. Now, no more of this talk, all right."

Kenna smiled. "Okay." She watched the tall man as he stood and put on his coat. The glow that seemed to radiate from him left her in awe.

❄ ❄ ❄

Kenna had just finished changing when she heard a noise coming from outside. She went to the front room, opened the door and froze.

Matthew was on the ground fighting off a large mountain lion. Seeing the blood covering him brought her out of shock and she screamed.

Matthew yelled, "Kenna, get my gun . . . under my bed! Hurry!"

Kenna ran through the front room back to his bedroom. She dropped to her hands and knees and frantically felt for the gun. Her father had taken her shooting frequently as a kid so she knew how to use a gun.

The pistol chambers were full and the safety was on, and she sent up a prayer of thanks that it was already loaded.

Kenna ran back out just in time to see the animal knock Matthew down again and claw at his face. She aimed shakily at the mountain lion and pulled the trigger. Her shot was true and the animal fell. She slid the gun across the wood floor in the front room and ran down to Matthew. There were huge gashes on his face, chest, and neck, and he was covered in blood, but he was still breathing.

"Matthew!" she cried, kneeling over the big man. "I don't know what to do!" She needed to get him inside, but she knew she couldn't do it alone. She didn't even know what to do if she *did* get him in.

Matthew opened his eyes slightly and tried to sit up. It took some major doing, but he managed to crawl to the porch and pull himself up enough for Kenna to help him up the stair and into the house.

Kenna cried as she helped him to lie down and saw the full extent of his injuries.

"I don't know what to do, Matthew!" she said, holding his bloody hand and sobbing.

Matthew's raspy voice filled the room. "Trust God . . . trust God, my Kenna. He will help you."

She quickly dropped to her knees by the bed and prayed. And just as quickly, she knew what she needed to do.

❊ ❊ ❊

Two hours later, Kenna dumped the bowl of bloody water down the sink, put the needle, thread, scissors, and the rest of the bandages away, and sat beside the unconscious man, holding his bandaged hand. Her mind kept repeating the same prayer over and over.

Please don't let him die, God. Please don't let him die. Matthew said Christmas is a time of miracles. I know you have already given me one . . . and I know I don't deserve it, but . . . please let me have just this one more and I will never ask for another thing.

Please don't let this angel die.

❄ ❄ ❄

Andrew smiled and wiped a tear away. The story never grew old. He was five the first time he heard it, and twenty years later, it still affected him the same. His eyes were again filled with awe as he gazed at his mother. "And did God save him?" he finally asked yet again.

Kenna pulled her eyes away from her son and rested them on her husband. She lifted her hand and reverently touched the scars above his neatly-trimmed beard.

Matthew kissed his wife's hand and answered for her. "He saved us both, son. He saved us both."

A Most Precious Gift

Tell me the story, Mama!" came the excited cry of the child bouncing up and down in front of the large, beautiful Christmas tree.

"All right," the mother laughed, trying to calm her eight year old son. Every Christmas Eve she told him the beloved story and it never seemed to get old to him. She sat on the sofa and the boy sat next to her, intently looking at her with excitement in his eyes. She smiled and began.

* * *

Once upon a time there was a young couple who lived in a small wooden house on the poor side of town. The couple didn't have many material things, but they always seemed to have what they needed and were very happy. Their only friends were the neighbors who lived in the poor section, for the rich were too proud to associate with them.

One day the couple was blessed with a baby. They named him Gabriel, and he was the most beautiful and perfect baby anyone had ever seen. Since the couple didn't have much, friends and neighbors gave homemade blankets, quilts, and clothes as gifts to them. The mother also made clothes for their son from scraps she managed to acquire here and there.

Through the years Gabriel grew to be a very special little boy. He was helpful to everyone around him and touched the hearts of all he came in contact with, which was only the people in the part of town he lived in.

When Gabriel turned eight, he asked his mother and father if he could venture into the rich side of town. The parents told Gabriel of their worry for him.

"The people will not be accepting of you," his mother said.

"They will be cruel," his father added sadly.

Gabriel smiled lovingly at his parents. "Everything will be fine," he said confidently.

The next day when his schoolwork and chores were done, Gabriel walked into the main part of town. Because his clothes weren't as nice as the other children, he was teased as he walked down the immaculate streets, but he held his head up high and greeted everyone with his beautiful smile.

Walking by one home, he spotted a couple of boys his age tromping through a lovely flowerbed. When an old woman burst through her front door yelling at the boys, they laughed and took off running. The old woman knelt in the flowerbed and cried.

"Please don't cry," Gabriel said, entering the woman's yard and kneeling down beside her.

"Who are you and what do you want?" the old woman grumbled.

"My name is Gabriel," he answered with a smile. He leaned forward and straightened one of the flowers. "I would like to help you fix your flower garden." He dug his fingers around another flower and straightened it.

The old woman turned up her nose. "You look like a beggar and I refuse to give you anything."

"I do not want anything, ma'am. I only want to help."

She looked at him suspiciously. "Why would you choose to help me without pay?"

Gabriel again smiled. "Because I love you."

"Hah!" the woman cried with a laugh. "You don't even know me."

Gabriel looked at the mashed flowers. "You like beautiful things. I can tell you are a good lady because you planted these flowers."

The old woman softened. She looked at Gabriel's innocent face for another moment, then she smiled. "I guess it would be all right if you helped me."

So Gabriel spent the next two hours helping the woman. When they were finished she offered to pay him, but Gabriel would not accept payment.

"But you have to let me give you something, the woman insisted.

Gabriel lifted his blue eyes to her face and said, "Your friendship will be enough." When the old woman pressed a wrinkled hand to his face, he smiled, then turned and headed back home.

The next day Gabriel noticed a baker unloading some bags of flour from a truck and carrying them into the bakery.

"Let me help you," Gabriel offered softly, picking up a bag of flour.

"I don't need your help," the man snapped. "Take your begging somewhere else."

"But I am not asking for pay, sir. I only want to help."

"Why?" asked the man curiously, his angry brow straightening.

"Because I love you," Gabriel answered innocently.

"You don't even know me," the man said, suspiciously.

Gabriel smiled, his blue eyes twinkling merrily. "I can tell you like good things because you make such delicious breads for your customers."

The corners of the baker's mouth turned up in a smile. "All right," he said. "You can help."

For the next hour Gabriel helped the baker unload the flour and organize the baking supplies in the storage room in back. When they were finished, the baker offered to pay Gabriel in both money and pastries, but Gabriel refused payment.

"But I have to pay you something," the baker said.

Gabriel lifted his kind eyes to the man's face and said, "Your friendship will be enough." When the man smiled and nodded, Gabriel shook his hand and headed back home.

❄ ❄ ❄

And so it went. Not a day passed that Gabriel didn't help someone in some way. From helping a worker keep the community park clean, to helping a building owner make repairs, to finding a lost pet for a child that had never shown him even an ounce of kindness, he always served in any way he could.

And his reply to the repeated question, "Why?" was always the same: "Because I love you."

After a while, people began to treat Gabriel differently. Oh, there were still those who were too proud and arrogant to acknowledge the young boy, but the ones he touched with his simple acts of kindness were in turn kind to him and his family. Since Gabriel always refused to accept pay, the people of the town began to show their gratitude for him by anonymously leaving boxes of food or
clothes on their porch. They invited Gabriel and his parents to their homes, and they even made him the honorary lighter of the huge Christmas tree in the town square that year, which was an important and very coveted job.

The years quickly passed and Gabriel was soon blessed with a sister that he loved very much. And other than helping his parents to care for his sister, nothing had changed. He still spent his leisurely hours helping others.

Gabriel soon grew from a boy into a man. When he turned twenty-five, he met a girl that he grew to love with all his heart and soul, and in August of that year they were married.

During the year that passed the people started seeing less and less of Gabriel. This was because he
got a job in a factory in the neighboring town. Now that he had a family, he had responsibilities to take care of.

Some of the townspeople began to gossip, upset that he was no longer coming into town to help them like he used to. Some said that he no longer cared about them. A few suggested that since he seemed to have

turned his back on them, perhaps the town should turn its back on him. However, some
of the people truly loved Gabriel and would never turn on him. They knew his heart and knew he hadn't
forgotten about the people of the town.

The mayor of the town decided that the real test would be Christmas Eve. It would be here in less than a week and Gabriel was still the honorary lighter of the town Christmas tree. They would just see
if he showed up.

Christmas Eve arrived and the time soon came for the lighting of the tree. All the townspeople were gathered around the tree. Gabriel's parents were there, as well as his young wife who sat in a chair
in front because she was expecting their first child.

The people waited and waited, but Gabriel still hadn't come. A low murmuring began to roll through the crowd.

"I knew he wouldn't come," an old man grumbled.

"You see, he doesn't care about us anymore!" another voice shouted suddenly.

Gabriel's wife stood and let her eyes move around the crowd. "My husband does care about you all," she said with conviction. "If he is able, he will be here."

But Gabriel never came.

* * *

The next morning the townspeople gathered at the large church located across the square from the Christmas tree. The murmuring that abound among the townspeople the night before was now replaced
by worry, for there was still no word from Gabriel. The people looked around the congregation and noticed that Gabriel's family was not present and they became even more worried. Just as the mayor had made the

decision to send someone out to Gabriel's home, his wife entered, followed by his parents. All three had tears in their eyes and their faces were solemn.

Gabriel's wife walked up the aisle to the front of the church to face the congregation. She stood looking at them quietly and everyone anxiously waited for her to speak, knowing now that something had happened. Even the people who grumbled against Gabriel the most looked at her anxiously. Finally, with a broken voice, she spoke.

"A policeman from the next town came to see me this morning. It seems that there was a string of robberies there last night and the men responsible were heading here. On his way home, Gabriel happened to walk by a house they had just robbed and heard their plan to come to our town and rob our homes. The men saw him and grabbed him before he could get away. He tried to talk them out of coming here, and they in turn tried to force him to join them. One of the men felt guilty and told him the only way he would live is if he joined them. He knew the other men would never let Gabriel leave alive. Again Gabriel refused. The men were eventually caught, but only after they had taken Gabriel's life."

The congregation sat in stunned and shocked silence. Of all the things that could have happened, they never imagined this. And all of this had happened while they stood around the tree grumbling and complaining about Gabriel, the man who had give more to their town than anyone. He'd never asked for anything except friendship, but he had given everything he could to the people and the town. And it was at that moment that they all finally began to realize how selfish they had been.

Gabriel's wife's final words fervently broke through their thoughts and touched their hearts forever, causing them to never be the same.

"The man who felt guilty about what happened said that before Gabriel died, he asked Gabriel why he was willing to sacrifice his life for the people of this town. And Gabriel replied soberly, "Because I love them.""

❄ ❄ ❄

"So the town realized that Gabriel gave them a precious gift that day. He gave them all he had. It was a Christmas that completely changed the town and one they never forgot."

"He was like Jesus, wasn't he, Mama?" the little boy said, looking into his mother's eyes.

"Yes, he was. If there was ever anyone who was a perfect example of Christlike love, it was him."

The boy looked at his mother thoughtfully. "I'm going to be just like him. Do you think I can, Mama?"

She smiled at her son. "Yes, you can, little Gabriel. After all, you are your father's son."

Author Bio

J. (Jewel) Adams stays crazy busy with her family and writing. She has written several books in different genres and is also a motivational speaker to both youth and adult audiences. She home schools her four kids that are still at home, and between that and conjuring up new ideas for her books, her brain is completely fried most of the time. She and her husband Sean are the parents of eight children, which means they are both losing hair, but hey, that's what Rogaine is for, right?

In her spare time (when she has any) she likes to curl up with a good book and a healthy stash of orange Tic Tacs. She and her family reside in Utah.

Jewel loves hearing from her fans, so if you would like to contact her to tell her how much you love her books or give her sympathy for the fried brain, or suggestions for the hair loss problem (for her husband, of course) contact her at **jewela40@gmail.com**

Website: **JewelAdams.com**

Blog: **jewelsbestgems.blogspot.com**

Other books by J. Adams/Jewel Adams
The Legacy
The Wishing Hour
Tears of Heaven
Place In This World
The Journey
Against the Odds
Mercedes' Mountain
Ebooks
The Wishing Hour
The Legacy
Tears of Heaven
Place In This World: The Sequel to The Journey
The Journey
Mercedes' Mountain
For Love of Angel (PDF only)
Elise's Heart (PDF only)
Children's Book
Forbidden Portals: The Quicksilver Project

All Books Are Also Available in Kindle and Nook Versions (Elise's Heart and Mercedes' Mountain excluded)